MW01135288

Table of Contents

Chapter 1 – Grand Opening on Wheels

"How are you today?" Heather asked her assistants as they crowded into the Donut Delights – Key West kitchen to help make the new flavor of the week.

"If anyone says berry good I'm going to groan so loud it deafens everyone here," her best friend Amy said.

The assistants laughed. Janae responded, "I was going to say that I was hungry today, but that's because I was saving room for the new donuts."

"Always a wise idea," Luz agreed.

"And that berry pun sounds like one of your old jokes anyway," Digby said, teasing Amy.

She ran with the setup and said, "It might have been a pun I used to make, but now I know I *cran* do better."

"What's the new flavor?" Nina asked.

"As you might have guessed from this silly wordplay," Heather said. "Our new flavor is the Cranberry Glazed Donut."

Her four assistants and her bestie licked their lips in anticipation, and Heather revealed a baker's sheet of the red donuts. She let

4

them each take a sample, and she explained how she came to create it.

"I was having a lot of trouble cooking sides for Thanksgiving this year."

"Her potatoes were pota-noes," Amy said.

The others were too busy eating their Cranberry Glazed snacks to sigh or groan at the jest.

"And so, I ended up sticking to what I was good with and making festive donuts for the meal, but it also inspired me to want to try other recipes with cranberries as well," Heather said. "I know that cranberries can be somewhat tart."

"But it's balanced so nicely here," Luz said. "It doesn't taste tart at all."

"The cake base is cranberry flavored, and then it's surrounded by a sweet glaze," Heather said. "And I made sure it was a vibrant red color to look appealing."

"It's funny because a red light means stop," said Amy. "But I don't think I can stop eating these delicious things."

"We're going to have to stop eating long enough to make some more," Heather said.

"I can get behind that," said Digby.

"And we need to move quickly," Heather said. "It's a busy day."

"That's right," said Amy, stopping her snacking long enough to explain. "It's the grand opening of the Mobile Groom Room."

Amy's boyfriend Jamie had been trying to start his own pet grooming business and was finally able to do so with the help of Heather's shop's investor: Rudolph Rodney. He had helped Jamie get his business situated, and today he would be taking his mobile grooming business on the road – or at least around some roads of Key West.

"Jamie promised to bring the van by this morning so we can wish it well," Heather said. "But he has to come by early so he can start his workday."

"And I want to have some of these donuts ready so that I can give them to him," Amy said. "He deserves them on his first day."

They all set to work and were able to create enough donuts to fill their display cases before Jamie drove by. Rudolph Rodney arrived as soon as the shop opened and he waited with them

to greet the van, happily enjoying
a donut.

The large Mobile Groom Room
parked on the street and Jamie
came out to greet them. He had a
huge smile on his face and was
practically skipping.

"I know I should be nervous,"
Jamie said. "But I'm just too
excited to be."

"You have nothing to be nervous
about, my boy," Rudolph Rodney
said. "I believe we've taken care
of everything that you need to get
started. You've worked very hard
to get to this point, and I'm
proud."

"Me too," Amy said, squeezing his hand.

"I'm also proud of myself," Rudolph Rodney admitted. "Investing in both you and Donut Delights. I must be a genius."

He chuckled to himself and then went in search of another celebratory donut, allowing Jamie to have a moment with his significant other and his friend.

"We prepared some donuts for you," Amy said. "And I didn't steal any either. I figured you needed all the energy you could get on a busy first day."

"It is going to be busy," Jamie said. "I have three bookings this morning where I'm going to customer's homes. I'll park on the street in front of their house and give their pets a bath. And then I'm permitted to park by the dog park this afternoon, and I think I'll get some customers there."

"I'm sure you will," Heather said. "Dave and Cupcake can get dirty at the park. Especially if it rained the day before like it did here."

"I had an idea," Jamie said. "I know it's late notice. But I was thinking that maybe I should get some donuts to have in the van while I'm at the park. I could let customers have something to snack on while they're waiting for their dog to finish their bath."

"That does seem like a nice idea," Amy said. "I should have thought of it before."

"It won't be a problem," Heather said. "We'd just have to wrap them individually, so there's no chance of any soap getting on them. But we could make them."

"It seems silly because you're the one in the van," Amy said. "But we could deliver them to you at the park."

"It'll be perfect," Heather said. "Because I've thought that Dave and Cupcake could use a bath too. We'll exchange donuts for grooming."

"It's a deal," Jamie said. "Well, I better get going."

They wished him good luck. Amy gave him a kiss, and then Jamie drove off to his first appointment.

Amy turned to her friend who had a thoughtful look on her face.

"What's going on?" Amy asked. "Don't tell me that you're having one of your bad feelings and that something terrible is going to happen. I don't want any crime to interfere with Jamie's grand opening."

Heather laughed. "No. I wasn't thinking anything like that. I was thinking whether I could make some donuts that are just for dogs and cats. I know Dave is crazy about all of my donuts."

"And his waistline still shows it," Amy said.

"Luckily, a dog on the beach he doesn't have to worry about a bikini figure," Heather said. "But I might still be able to make some specifically doggie donuts."

"Let's focus on the human ones first," Amy said. "I want to eat some more, and then see the new van in action."

Chapter 2 – Parked in the Park

"It looks like he's doing well," Amy said, proudly.

"Based on those tail wags, I'd agree," said Heather.

They had arrived at the dog park and saw the van in the nearby parking lot. A clean and happy golden retriever was walking away from it with his owner.

The van was metallic gray but had been decorated to make it more festive. Amy had helped with the artwork, and it now had adorable cartoon pictures of sudsy puppies frolicking around the side of the van. The doors to the vehicle were open, and it was surprisingly roomy and functional.

There were two bath areas. One was on the ground for large dogs, and one was at a counter level for smaller pets. There were cabinets and baskets that were filled with supplies. There was also a small waiting area where a pet could sit behind a gate and stay clean. There was one dog with long white hair in that area.

Jamie looked up from cleaning the tub that the golden retriever had splashed in and waved at his friends.

Amy's arms were filled with boxes of donuts, and Heather's hands were holding leashes, so they hurried over to say hello instead of waving back. Dave, the dog, was happy to see Jamie and jumped right into the van greet him and get his tummy rubbed. The kitten Cupcake was more dubious about all the water in the room.

Amy deposited the donuts in the front of the van. She moved closer to hug her boyfriend, but then paused when she saw how damp his clothes were. Instead, she kissed him on the cheek.

"Good first day?" Heather asked.

"It's been great," Jamie said. "All my morning appointments promised to recommend me to their friends. One cat was a little tricky, but otherwise, the grooming was smooth. And I had few people visit me at the park already."

"We saw one happy customer," Heather said.

"I think the artwork on the side of the van entices people to come see what I offer. Thanks, Ames," Jamie said, grinning at his girlfriend.

"Well, you know, I do what I can," Amy said nonchalantly.

"We brought the Cranberry Glazed Donuts. They're all wrapped up tight and ready to give out," Heather said.

"Thanks," Jamie said. "And are you here for grooming as well?"

Cupcake seemed to realize what was being asked and hid behind Heather. She bent down and picked the grumpy kitten up.

"We are if you're not too busy," Heather said. "It looks like you have a client in the corner."

"That is Miss Marshmallow," Jamie said. "Her owner must be running late. She asked if it was all right to leave her here while

she ran an errand, but she was
very specific about the grooming.
She said her dog was her best
friend."

Dave realized that they were
talking about someone other than
him and went over to investigate.
He sniffed at the gate and
wagged his tail. Miss
Marshmallow seemed
unimpressed. She looked away.

Dave put his paw on the gate and
made a playful little noise. Miss
Marshmallow laid down and
ignored him. Her silky hair
blocked him from her view.

Dave looked up at Heather, and
she shrugged. Sometimes she

and her dog understood each other perfectly. Usually, this was because Dave was asking for donuts, but she sensed what he was feeling now. He was confused why the lady dog didn't want to be his friend.

Cupcake's feelings were even more clear, and it was evident that she did not want to take a bath. However, Jamie eventually calmed her down. He soothed her and gave her a bath that she didn't completely hate.

Dave spent the whole time trying to impress the unimpressed Miss Marshmallow, and not getting so much as a tail wag or sniff in response. Dave enjoyed his soapy bath though, and both of Heather's pets enjoyed a donut treat at the end of it for good behavior.

When Heather's pets were all groomed, Miss Marshmallow's owner had still not returned.

"She must be running really late," Heather said. "I guess that happens sometimes though. When we investigate leads, it sometimes takes much longer than we expect."

"Especially if we're running and hiding for our lives," Amy commented.

"I'm sure she'll be back soon," Jamie said. "It didn't seem like she wanted to be away from her dog for very long."

"Just as long as this isn't some kind of ploy to get us to adopt a dog right now," Amy said. "We're not planning on getting for a while. Not until things settle down."

"It's no ploy," Jamie said.

"You might say that even if it were a ploy," Amy said suspiciously.

"I don't think Miss Marshmallow is exactly the sort of dog that we'd pick as our best friend," Jamie said. "She'd be high maintenance and might not like the lifestyle we lead."

"You mean running off to bakeries and crime scenes?" Amy asked.

"Exactly," said Jamie.

"I'm not sure how well she'd get along with the other animals either," Heather said. "Dave seems taken with her, but she's not giving him the time of day. And relationships between dogs and cats can be strained as it is."

"Luckily, it's not a ploy," Amy said, giving Jamie a hard look.

He held up his hands. "It's not. Miss Marshmallow's owner should be any minute to pick up her best friend."

They were all satisfied with this response, but that night proved what he said to be wildly untrue.

Chapter 3 – A Surprise Guest

Dave jumped to attention.

"The movie isn't over yet, buddy," Heather said.

After a busy day, Heather and her family were relaxing at home. Cupcake was cuddling with her daughter Lilly, and Dave was in between Heather and her husband, Ryan. He was a detective with the Key West Police Force, but luckily, because he wasn't currently investigating a case, he was able to come home in time to watch a movie. Amy had joined them because Ryan wasn't home yet and because there were sure to be more donuts at Heather's gatherings.

Amy looked up from her half-eaten donut at the direction Dave was pointing. He was facing the door.

"Do you think Jamie is home?" Amy asked. They lived in an adjoining house above the Shepherd's place, so he would be nearby when he arrived home.

Lilly jumped up and brought Cupcake to the window with her.

"His van is here," she said. "It looks so cool! I want to visit it when it's open sometime too."

"We'll visit again when you're not in school," Heather promised. "Our pets have never looked better than after that bath."

At hearing the word bath, Cupcake jumped out of Lilly's arms and found a safe space to hide.

"He's getting something from the back of the van," Lilly said. "Uh oh."

"Uh on?" asked Amy.

"He's not alone," Lilly said.

The adults barely had time to ask who would be arriving at this time of night, when Jamie entered. In his arms was Miss Marshmallow.

"It was a ploy!" Amy said.

"No," Jamie said. "I wasn't trying to sneak another dog into our lives. I just didn't know what to do. Her owner never came to pick her up."

Dave ran over to greet Jamie and Miss Marshmallow. Jamie set her own the ground, and she pawed at his leg. She looked unhappy with her new surroundings.

Lilly held her hand out for the new dog to smell her, and she grudgingly let the girl pet her fur. She must have found it comforting because she kept close to Lilly's side.

"What happened?" Heather asked.

"I've been by the park all this time," Jamie said. "I was waiting for her owner to come, but it got so dark and was so late, I figured it was time to come home. I had water and a few treats, but I didn't have dog food for a meal in the van. I thought she might be getting hungry."

"I'll show her where the food is," Lilly said.

She showed their four-legged guest to the kitchen, followed by

Dave who was eager to show off his food bowl.

"Is it possible she was abandoning the dog with you?" Ryan asked.

"I wouldn't think so," Jamie said. "You should have seen how devoted she was to the dog when she dropped her off for a bath. They had been playing at the park and then saw the van. She said it worked out because she could run her errand and then pick up the dog, instead of having to drop her off at home first. I think the dog is actually a bit spoiled."

"Well," Heather said. "Many of us end up spoiling our pets. I can't resist giving Dave donuts when I see his puppy dog eyes."

"Miss Marshmallow has a tag on her collar, but it only says the dog's name and a phone number. I called and left messages, but she never picked up," Jamie said.

"So, you decided to bring her here?" Amy asked.

"I think I'll go back to the park tomorrow so she could find me again," Jamie said. "I have flyers around town, but I don't know if she knows how to get in contact with me."

"I think returning to where she last knew you were is a good idea," Heather said.

"But I also wanted to check in with you, Ryan," Jamie said. "I was afraid something might have happened to her. You haven't heard anything, have you?"

"I'm not investigating any murders right now if that's what you mean," said Ryan. "First thing in the morning, I can check with hospitals and make sure that she isn't there. And I'll make sure that she hasn't contacted us."

"Right," Amy said. "She might be afraid that her pup was dognapped."

"I did wait for hours," Jamie said.

"What you've done makes perfect sense," Ryan said. "And I'm sure we'll get it all sorted out in the morning."

"I hope so," said Jamie. "I don't know her name or anything about her except that has a dog and doesn't answer the phone number on the license. She paid with cash, so I don't have any credit card information in my system."

"We might have to change your business plan," Amy joked. "We can't have you getting paid with abandoned dogs."

"I just don't think she abandoned Miss Marshmallow," Jamie said. "You can tell when people really care about their pets and she really did. Maybe I'm overreacting. Maybe she just got held up and will find Miss Marshmallow tomorrow."

"This does make for an exciting first day," said Amy. "I hope the second day is calmer."

"Me too," said Jamie. "I hope we don't find out bad news."

Heather was also starting to get a bad feeling about what had happened, but she pushed the feelings away. She told Jamie that they would be happy to feed

Miss Marshmallow, but that it might be better for her if she stayed upstairs. That way Dave wouldn't bother her by trying to impress her. Amy reluctantly agreed.

"Let's take care of the dog and not say anything to upset Lilly tonight," said Heather. "We'll figure out what happened in the morning."

They made sure that Miss Marshmallow was fed and then Amy and Amy started to leave with her.

"I just hope this isn't a trick," Amy said to her friend.

"I just hope it isn't foul play," said Heather.

Chapter 4 – Lost Owner

"They say cranberry juice is very good for you," Leila said. "Let's assume that the donuts are too."

"I don't need an excuse to eat these wonderful treats," Eva laughed.

Heather was happy to see her favorite customers at Donut Delights. The two senior ladies had moved from Texas to Key West to continue being her neighbors, and they were now all good friends. The ladies were also huge fans of Heather's donuts and were not shy about complimenting them.

Amy usually joined in the donut discussions of deliciousness, but today was yawning.

"Are you all right, dear?" Eva asked, taking a moment away from her snack to inquire about her friend.

"Just tired," Amy said. "That Marshmallow mutt kept me up all night. She didn't seem to think the blankets we put down were soft enough. She kept pawing them and looking up at me with disdain."

"A dog was looking up at you with disdain?" Eva asked.

"This one was," said Amy. "And she kept looking out the window and whining. I guess she misses her owner, so I could kind of understand it. But why did she need to make us miss her all night too?"

"Ryan said he didn't have any luck tracking her down at the local hospitals," Heather said.

"Which sounds like a good thing," Leila said. "That she's not in the hospital."

"Right," Heather said, hoping that was true. "Do you know if Jamie had any luck at the park? Maybe she did return this morning."

"I haven't heard anything," Amy said. "But I might have told him not to talk to me until he got rid of the furball."

"So, she probably didn't come in yet," Heather thought aloud.

"Are we sure there even is an owner?" Amy asked. "Did anyone see her besides Jamie? Maybe this is all a big charade in order to get me to welcome to poor lost puppy into our home."

"I thought you were warming up to the idea of your own dog," Heather said.

"I am. But warming and not boiling over with enthusiasm,"

Amy said. "I always loved Dave. And after that case that Jamie and I had to dog-sit a witness, I've been more open to the idea. But I don't want to rush into anything. What if a dog would get in the way of our investigations? And what if I want to move cross-country again?"

"Well, last time I moved cross-country I took my pets and all my friends along," Heather said with a smile.

"You can't keep us away," Eva agreed.

"And this dog is not the right dog for us," Amy said.

"What's wrong with her?" asked Leila.

"She's prissy, and caring for her hair takes longer than caring for mine," Amy began.

"But Jamie is a professional groomer," Heather pointed out.

"And," Amy said. "I tried to give her a donut to quiet her. And she wouldn't take it."

"She wouldn't take it?" asked Eva in shock.

"She doesn't like donuts?" asked Leila, equally aghast.

"All right," Heather said. "I think we need to find this owner. Let's check in with Jamie, and if she hasn't arrived yet, we're going to do what we do best."

"Eat the donuts that the dog doesn't want?" Amy suggested.

"The other thing we do best," said Heather. "Investigate."

***

"I'm worried," Jamie said. "If you had seen her when she dropped off Miss Marshmallow you'd be concerned too. She wouldn't have abandoned her dog."

"Yes. But we didn't see her," Amy said. "Did anybody else see her?"

"I'm not trying to trick you," Jamie sighed. "Don't you believe me?"

"Fine," Amy said. "I guess I trust you. But maybe it's nicer to think that you were trying to con me into getting a dog, rather than something bad happened to a nice lady that puts up with a prissy pooch."

"I knew you wouldn't waste the police's time on something false," Heather said. "But so far, Ryan hasn't found anything to help. The cell phone was a burner phone. It can't be linked back to the owner."

"I wish there were more information I could give," Jamie said. "But all I have is the phone number and description. She was thin and average height. Blonde hair. I'd guess in her thirties."

"Is there anything else that you think might be helpful to add?" Heather asked.

"Well," Jamie said, thinking about it. "I did think at the time that was a little dressed up to be playing fetch in the park. She was wearing a dress, and her hair was pulled up in a fancy sort of bun. But after I met Miss Marshmallow, I thought maybe the two of them were just always at their most fashionable."

Miss Marshmallow made a noise when she heard her name. Amy walked up to the fenced-in area of the Mobile Groom Room van.

"Yeah. We're talking about you," Amy said. "It's all going to be all right though. Don't worry."

Miss Marshmallow laid down, sadly with her head on her paws. Amy grudgingly started patting her back.

Heather tried to focus on their case. "And she said she was going to run some errands?"

Jamie nodded. "She didn't say what it was. But she said it would be helpful if she could leave her dog here for a bit."

"Which direction did she go?" asked Heather.

"I think it was that way," Jamie said.

"Not towards the parking lot?" Heather asked.

"No," Jamie said. "Now that you mention it, I didn't see her head towards the cars."

"Then she didn't drive to her errand," Heather said. "It had to be somewhere within walking distance."

Amy scanned the area. "If we move away from the dog park, then she was either heading to that palm tree grove or to those shops down the road."

"Let's get moving," Heather said.

***

After visiting all the shops within walking distance and not finding out any information, Heather and Amy were feeling discouraged.

"I know it wasn't a thorough description," Heather said. "But I would have thought that someone would have recognized her if she went into a store yesterday."

"Maybe she didn't go into any of them," Amy said. "Maybe she walked that way and met someone on the street. Or she took a taxi. Or she did go to her car and Jamie didn't see her."

"You're right," Heather said. "She could have headed anywhere. We don't know anything about her to inform our opinion of where she went."

"She might even have been headed towards those palm trees," Amy said.

"It's worth checking it out," Heather said.

"But what errand could she be doing there?" asked Amy.

"If we find evidence that she was there, then that's something we'd need to figure out," said Heather. "And if there's no evidence that she was there, we'll have to think of something else. It is also possible that she was lying to Jamie."

They started walking among the trees. The ground was uneven, so it was hard to see too far in front of them. They rounded a bend and Amy said, "I think we found the evidence that she was here."

Then, Amy turned away, but Heather surveyed the scene. A blonde woman in a nice dress lay dead on the ground.

"You better call Ryan," Amy said.

"In just a moment," said Heather. "I think there's one other call I should make first."

She took out her cell phone and dialed the number that had been listed on Miss Marshmallow's collar. They heard a ringing sound coming from the dead woman's purse.

"I will call Ryan," Heather said. "And tell him that unfortunately, we found the missing owner."

Chapter 5 – Crime Scene Among the Palm Trees

Ryan and his partner Detective Peters arrived at the scene quickly.

"I can't believe you found her like this," Ryan said. "I should have taken the tip that Jamie gave us more seriously. I should have begun the search for her that night instead of in the morning."

"It's not your fault," Heather said. "At the time, she could have just been a late owner."

"But Jamie was suspicious," Ryan said.

"The medical examiner will tell us more," Heather said. "But I have a strong feeling that she was killed earlier in the afternoon. I think she only expected to be gone a little while and then would pick up her dog, but someone killed her and stopped her from following through with that plan."

"That does sound right," Ryan admitted. "The medical examiner took the body to conduct the autopsy. He should be able to give us a time of death soon."

"What do you know so far?" Heather asked.

"It looks like strangulation was the cause of death," said Ryan.

"It didn't look like there were marks in the shape of hands on her throat," Heather said.

"I agree," Ryan said. "The killer used a rope of some sort. Probably flatter than what we usually think of for rope."

"But why was she strangled?" Amy asked. "What was she doing here? She told Jamie she was going to run an errand, but what errand could she be running by these palm trees? Collecting coconuts?"

"She might have just said that she was running an errand," Heather said. "But it does appear that she came here on purpose.

And coming here led to her death."

"I don't have any ideas on this one," Amy said. "Was she planning on bringing her dog here and then decided against it? Was she really going to bring her dog home first and so she was supposed to come here later? Was she meeting someone? Did he kill her? Did she stumble onto something and that was the reason for killing her? I have a million questions and no answers. I don't like that."

"I think I have an answer," Detective Peters said, responding to them as he approached. He had been expanding the search around the crime scene for clues, and it looked as if he had found one.

"Did you find a clue to tell us who the killer is?" Amy asked.

"I think I found the murder weapon," Detective Peters said proudly. He was a young detective and was always pleased when he could prove that he was worthy of his badge.

"What is it?" Ryan asked.

"It's a dog leash," Detective Peters said. "I marked where it was dropped over there. I think the killer thought it might have been hidden in the sand and brush, but he didn't count on my keen eye. Because I keenly saw it. With my eyes."

He was afraid that he was talking too much and quickly handed the bag over to the other investigators to look it over.

"This isn't just any leash," Heather said. "I think it's Miss Marshmallow's. It matches her collar."

"Because Miss Marshmallow is a small dog, Jamie would give her a bath in the smaller tub. I don't think he would have kept her on the leash," Amy said.

"So most likely the victim had the leash with her," Heather said. "And then the killer took it and used it kill her."

"Do we know what the victim's name is?" Amy asked. "I don't like calling her the owner or the victim all the time."

"The identification in her purse says her name is Melanie Grayson," Ryan said.

"Was there anything else in her purse to give us a clue?" Heather asked.

"I'm afraid not," Ryan said. "She didn't keep very much in there. Most of what she had related to her dog. She kept dog brushes, treats, and baggies in there."

"Have we found anything that could help point us to her killer?" Heather asked.

"We did find some footprints," Detective Peters said.

"Unfortunately, the killer must have realized that he left footprints in the sand and tried to smear the prints. There are only partials left now," said Ryan. "However, if we have a shoe to compare them to, they might still be helpful."

"I'll keep examining the scene," Detective Peters said. "I already found the murder weapon. Maybe I'll find something just as exciting."

He went back to his search.

"I should join him," Ryan said.

Heather nodded. "Let us know what you find. We'll catch Jamie up on what's been happening. And then we can both look more into Melanie Grayson's life and see who would have a motive to kill her."

"Hopefully we can find out what she was doing here and then discover who the killer is," said Ryan. He said good luck and goodbye to Heather and Amy, and then went to join his partner.

"There are already so many questions in this case," Amy said. "But two are rising to the top for me."

"I'm guessing one is who killed her," said Heather.

"Right," said Amy. "And the other is what do we do with Miss Marshmallow?"

Chapter 6 – Going to the Dogs

"I think it's fun," Lilly said. "It's almost like a party."

Heather didn't quite share the same sentiments. She and Amy had been failing at finding something that would make Miss Marshmallow eat. While she had deigned herself to eat Dave's food the night before, today she would not be bothered.

Heather and Amy had tried several different types of dog food and treats that they had in the house, and then had resorted to human food. They had tried many foods that Dave and Cupcake had been overjoyed to sample, including chicken, fish, hamburger, and donuts. However, Miss Marshmallow had turned her nose up at all of them.

There was definitely enough food for it to be a party, and there were more animals in the house to make it seem like there were guests. However, the mood was not festive. Amy was getting cranky, and Heather wasn't far behind.

Heather forced herself to take a deep breath and then said, "She might just be sad because she misses her owner. Maybe she's not hungry right now."

"Fine," Amy said. "If we can stop focusing on what the dog is going to eat, then it's my turn. Hand me a donut."

Heather obliged and grabbed a donut for herself too.

Dave wasn't sure where to direct his attention. Torn between tasty meat dishes, his favorite donuts, and a pretty lady dog, he was spinning in circles. This did little to impress Miss Marshmallow.

Cupcake had been very leery of the new dog at first, but when Miss Marshmallow didn't seem eager to either bark or chase, she had calmed down. She was enjoying the food most of all.

"Ryan should be home any minute," Heather said. "And he might have some updates on the case."

"It will be nice to focus on the case again and not on the spoiled dog," said Amy. "If she doesn't want to eat, she doesn't have to."

There was a knock on the door and Jamie came into the kitchen to join them. He carried with him a bag of dog food that finally caused Miss Marshmallow to show some enthusiasm. He poured it into a bowl, and she devoured it quickly.

"What's that?" asked Amy.

"Ryan said he found the victim's address and did a quick search there. He called me to let me know the brand of dog food that he found there so I could pick some up," Jamie explained. "She seems to like it."

"What's in it?" Amy asked.

"It's a special health food blend," Jamie said. "Very fancy. It looks like there's a good amount of kale in it too."

Dave gave one sniff of the bag and ran away from it. He moved closer to Heather. He was more of a donut dog.

Ryan soon joined them. He looked around the room at all the types of food on the floor and counters. "A buffet tonight?"

"I guess it is," Heather said. "We were trying to find something that Miss Marshmallow would eat. And now we have our choice of meals."

Ryan picked up a hamburger, and the others grabbed some of the main course as well.

"I don't like the idea of eating what a dog rejected," Amy said.

"Maybe she didn't reject them," Jamie said. "Maybe she just

wanted the leftovers in a doggie bag."

Heather turned to Ryan. "You saved the day by finding her brand of food. Did you find out anything else while you were at her apartment?"

"It was actually a very impersonal apartment," Ryan said. "There were furniture and her clothes, but there were no pictures anywhere. The only thing that gave the apartment any personality were things that related to her dog. She had a fancy dog bed and lots of canine accessories."

"That's interesting," Heather said. "I wonder why she didn't have any mementos of her life besides things related to her dog."

"I wonder why there couldn't be a clue that would lead us to the killer," Amy said.

"That would make it too easy," said Jamie.

"Mom," Lilly said. "Do you mind if I take the pets to the backyard? Now that Miss Marshmallow ate she might be in a better mood."

"That's a great idea," Heather said.

She made sure that Lilly was all right with the animals in the yard. Dave was showing off by trying to jump and do tricks. Miss Marshmallow decided to sniff in the opposite direction instead.

Then, Heather returned to the kitchen. With Lilly out of the room, they could discuss the grittier details of the case.

"What other things did you find out?" Heather asked. "Did the medical examiner get back to you?"

"He did," Ryan said. "And it looks like your idea of the timeline was correct. He estimates that she was strangled between one and four p.m. the day before."

"She dropped Miss Marshmallow off at the van around two," Jamie said. "And she was definitely alive then."

"That helps us even more," Ryan said, putting his dinner down to write a note.

"And you think she was killed at that palm tree grove?" Heather asked. "She wasn't moved there?"

"We think she was killed there," Ryan agreed.

"Did Peters find anything else there?" asked Amy. "He was pretty excited."

"It's difficult because the crime happened outside," said Ryan. "The scene was exposed to the elements, and it was near a public area. However, we did find a hair near the body that doesn't belong to the victim. It's possible it belongs to the killer. We're running a check on it now to see if it belongs to anyone in the system."

"It would be really helpful if there were some DNA evidence at the scene," Heather said, hopefully.

"And there's that partial boot print," Amy reminded them. "If we have a suspect, we can compare him to the evidence to see if it's a match."

"We just need the suspect," Heather said.

"I did find out a little more about Melanie Grayson," Ryan said. "I found out she was working at an architecture firm in town."

"Then I think we know where we're going in the morning," Heather said. "We'll interview her coworkers."

"And maybe the architects could give us the blueprint plans on

how to solve this case," Amy
joked.

Chapter 7 – Any Answers from Architects

Heather and Amy arrived at Burdey Brothers Beach Homes with Detective Peters and Ryan. It was a small office building but captured the beachy theme spot-on. It looked more like an exotic vacation home than a workplace. That was probably what they wanted their customers to think when they came in.

"I know we came here to investigate a murder," Amy said. "But is they any chance we could look at their houses? We've had a lot of trouble with ours, and these look fantastic."

Heather had to admit that they did have many troubles with their building when they first moved in and their tropical home did require a lot of upkeep. However, she thought it would be unlikely that they would find another three-family home that would be perfect for housing Eva and Leila, the Shepherd family, and Amy and Jamie, and still have a backyard for the pets to play in. She also didn't want to be deterred from her investigation. She decided she needed to keep Amy on task too.

"The sooner we solve the case, the sooner you won't have to care for Miss Marshmallow anymore," Heather pointed out.

That kept Amy's attention, and she led the rest of the group right into the office. The first person they saw was a young woman with large glasses and a big smile.

"Hello," she said. "Are you looking for your dream home? Because Burdey Brothers Beach Homes will help you achieve that dream. Oh, wait. You have badges. You're police. What's going on?"

"Did a Melanie Grayson work here?" Ryan asked.

"Yes," the woman said. "She was an assistant like I was. But she didn't come to work today. Is she in trouble? Is she okay?"

"Why don't you tell us a little bit about yourself first?" Detective Peters said. "What's your name?"

"I'm Kim McConnell. I've worked here for about four years, and with Melanie for about two. What's going on?"

"Did you know her well?" Heather asked. "How would you describe her?"

"She was quiet," Kim said. "She was nice, but she didn't share a lot of personal details. Except about her dog. She loved Miss Marshmallow. She'd bring her to work whenever there wouldn't be clients stopping by. She was such a cheerful dog. We loved when she visited."

"You did?" Amy asked. "Would you like her to visit now and stay awhile? I wouldn't mind getting her out of my hands."

"Why would she visit?" Kim asked. "And it sounds like she'd be here without Melanie. Something is wrong. Melanie wouldn't leave Miss Marshmallow alone. What happened? Is she sick? Did someone hurt her?"

Kim was starting to look quite upset, and another coworker

noticed. He was a tall man with a bit of a paunch.

"What's going on here?" He asked, striding into the situation. "What are you saying to upset my employee?"

"You're in charge here?" Ryan asked.

"I'm one of the Burdey Brothers. So, yes, I'm one of the people in charge. I'm Jason Burdey. And I'd really like to know what's going on."

"It's about Melanie," Kim said. "They haven't told me what's wrong, but they have Miss Marshmallow."

Jason Burdey's hand moved to the wall for support. "She would never leave Miss Marshmallow alone."

"That's what I said," Kim replied.

Jason Burdey looked directly at Ryan. "Officer, is she dead?"

"I'm afraid we are investigating Melanie Grayson's murder," Ryan said. "And we'd like to find out all the information we can about her."

Jason Burdey paled. "Her murder... Will you excuse me for a minute?"

Without waiting for an answer, he hurried away towards the restroom. Heather suspected that the news turned his stomach. But was the reason for his illness because he was upset about losing a coworker and possible friend? Or was this the result of a guilty conscience?

"How was she killed?" Kim asked. "Do you know who did it? You're going to catch him, right?"

"It sounds like Jason is getting sick," a man said running up to them. He stopped when he noticed there were people there besides Kim. He was shorter than Jason but had the same hair and features. Heather suspected he was the other Burdey Brother.

"Officers, is there a problem?" he asked.

"Melanie was murdered," Kim said. "They want to know whatever we can tell them about her. She was so private, but…"

"Yes. Thank you. I'll take care of it from here." He turned to the investigators. "I'm Junior Burdey. Let me see what I can tell you about my employee. Let me find her file."

He started to lead the investigators to an office. It looked as if Kim was about to

protest, but he spoke instead.
"Tell Jason that we're very
serious about the New Year's
Eve Party rule. If he makes a
mess in the bathroom, he's the
one to have to clean it."

Then, he gave the investigators
his winning architect smile. He
realized the salesman side of
things might not be appropriate
for the proceedings and adjusted
to a stoic grim face.

He led them to the office.

"Now what would you like to
know?" Junior Burdey asked.

"Everything," said Heather. "Anything that might lead to us catching a killer."

Chapter 8 – Office Notes

Junior Burdey showed them into his office, which also looked like a tropical bungalow but had filing cabinets in it. It had a large window with a beautiful view of the ocean in the distance.

Junior opened a drawer and pawed through it, while the others looked at his seating arrangement. Because of a large waterfall fixture, there was only space for two small chairs. They all tried to be polite and offer them to each other.

Amy got bored of gesturing for one another to take the chair and plopped into one. She took out the tablet they used for taking notes and prepared to listen to the questioning. Heather thought that one of the detectives should sit because they were more official, but Ryan wanted to be a gentleman and refused. Detective Peters was feeling awkward about the situation and began admiring the art on the wall as an excuse to stop the exchange. Heather finally relented and sat down.

Junior Burdey turned around. Having missed all the quiet commotion, he sat down at this desk and faced the investigators.

"This is my personnel file on Melanie Grayson," he said. "She

was a good worker. I can't
believe she was involved in any
trouble. But you said she was
murdered?"

"I'm afraid so," Ryan said. "Now
what was her job here?"

"She was an assistant here,"
Junior explained. "Jason and I
design beach houses for clients,
and our assistants keep us on
track."

"And whose assistant was
Melanie's?" asked Heather.

"They both worked for both of
us," Junior said.

"Your brother seemed very upset by the news of Melanie Grayson's death," Detective Peters pointed out.

"It's upsetting to know that we lost a part of our team, especially in such a violent way," said Junior. "And he's always been a bit soft."

"Was she working on any projects that were giving you difficulty?" Ryan asked.

"Do you mean could one of our projects have been related to her murder?" Junior asked. "I don't see how. We just design beach homes here. There's nothing sinister about that. And we haven't had any unhappy clients."

"What do you have in her file?" Ryan asked.

"Not much," Junior said, pushing the file towards them. "We never had to fill out any incident reports about her. This is just her information from when she was hired. I have her resume in here too. She worked in a few offices before this one. It looks like she moved from Atlanta."

"Did she ever tell you why she moved?" Heather asked.

"No," Junior said. "She didn't talk much about her personal life. Not that we would encourage that sort of thing in the office. We did focus more on our business here. I do know that she had a dog."

"I wonder if her move has any bearing on what happened," Heather said.

"Maybe she just wanted to be closer to the beach," Amy said.

"A lot of our business comes from clients wanting exactly that," said Junior.

"Did Melanie Grayson come to work on Monday?" asked Ryan.

"Yes," answered Junior. "But that was her half day. She leaves at one on Mondays. Kim leaves early on Thursdays. The rest of the week is a typical nine to five."

"And you didn't think it was odd that she didn't show up yesterday?" Heather asked.

"I wasn't quite sure that she didn't request the day off. Her friends were covering for her. And she did have to take some time off before when her dog got sick," Junior said.

"Does she get sick a lot?" asked Amy.

Junior didn't know the answer or the relevance to the case and shrugged.

"Where were you Monday between two and four?" asked Ryan.

"I was still at work. Jason and Kim were both here with me," he said.

"And how did Melanie Grayson seem that day?" Heather asked. "Did she seem nervous or worried about anything?"

"It seemed like a normal day at work. The assistants are always a bit happier on their half days, and she acted like things were fine," Junior said. "But she was always a very private person. She didn't share very much about herself here at the office. Here's her file. I'm sorry we can't be of any more help."

He was about to show them out, when Heather said, "I think there is one more thing that could be of help. Does she have a desk here?"

Junior nodded and led her back into the room where they had met Kim. Melanie Grayson's desk was opposite from Kim's, both spatially in the room and in décor. Kim's desk had novelty office supplies with references to her favorite shows, there were pictures of her friends and family, and there were trinkets from places she visited. Melanie Grayson's desk was stiff and impersonal. The only thing that she had added to the workplace supplies was a picture of Miss Marshmallow.

"It's just like her apartment," Detective Peters said. "That might have been a hotel room because there was nothing there to mark it as a certain individual's."

"Except for the dog stuff," Amy added.

"You're welcome to take anything that you think might be relevant," Junior said. "I don't know how it could be, but I'm not a detective."

"Thank you," said Ryan.

Kim returned to the room, but Junior sent her off on an errand. "These detectives might take some paperwork from Melanie's desk. Could you make sure we have copies of the Pasquale contracts and the Sanderson blueprints?"

Kim nodded and walked away. Junior eventually left too to check in his brother.

Most of the paperwork on the desk was strictly business related. There were blueprints and contracts and permits.

"We can sort through this more at the station," Ryan said. "And make sure that none of these projects could be related to her death."

Heather nodded. "Though if I were upset about a dream house I bought that turned into a nightmare, I'd be more upset with the architect than with his assistant."

They continued going through the drawers and piles of papers, until Heather saw something that was as red as her Cranberry Glazed Donuts. It was a paper heart cut out of red construction paper.

"Looks like we found something personal," Amy commented.

"And a clue," Heather said. "Look at that message."

It read: Meet me by the trees in the park when you get off work.

Chapter 9 – Barks and Backgrounds

"That's weird though, right?" Amy asked.

"I think it means that the killer suspected we might check for prints if we found the note," Heather said.

Heather and Amy had come to the police station to see the results of Ryan's fingerprint test on the love note that they had found in Melanie's desk. Unfortunately, the only prints on it were the victim's.

"I knew I shouldn't have gotten my hopes up," Amy said. "But fingerprints on the note sure would have been helpful."

Even Miss Marshmallow had been disappointed by this turn of events. They had brought her to the station with them, and she had been pacing back and forth. Heather had thought that getting her away from adoring Dave and suspicious Cupcake would be good for her, but she was still antsy.

"I love when you bring donuts into the station, but you're bringing pets now?" a voice asked.

They turned and saw Chief Chet approaching them. He was the most laidback police chief that

Heather had ever encountered and was normally seen in shorts and sandals. Today was no exception, but he was also wearing a pair of novelty sunglasses. He pushed them up on his head to look at the dog.

"She's a witness in a murder case," Ryan explained. "This was the victim's dog. And she's one of the last living things to see Melanie Grayson before she was killed."

"Jamie is one of the others," Amy said. "And he's not feeling too happy about that. He's been feeling guilty about it happening so close to his van, and he wasn't able to help."

"That's not his fault," Heather said. "It was too far away for him to hear anything, and there's no way he could have known what was happening at the time. He's also done everything he can to care for her dog now."

"Maybe you can tell him that," Amy suggested.

If Chief Chet was annoyed by having animals in the station, it was soon forgotten. He began petting Miss Marshmallow and soon found himself talking baby talk to the dog.

"Who's the pwettiest widdle pupdog? That would be you. Yes, it would. Yes, it would," he cooed.

Miss Marshmallow seemed to enjoy the attention. It took all of Ryan and Detective Peters's willpower not to laugh. Heather covered up hers with a cough.

Chief Chet stood up and assumed his power position again. "This little lady is welcome to visit anytime."

"Thanks," Amy said. "But we're hoping to solve the case soon and find out who she belongs to now."

"The victim doesn't have any family?" Chief Chet asked.

"Not that we can find," said Ryan.

"But her background does seem odd," Heather commented. "No one seems to know very much about her."

"And I've begun a background check on her," Ryan said. "There's very little about her before she came to Key West two years ago. There's almost nothing on record."

"And we find this suspicious?" Chief Chet asked.

"Because she was murdered, everything is suspicious," said Ryan.

"What about that resume that Junior Burdey gave us?" asked

Heather. "He said that she worked in offices before so it should have information on it."

"I checked some of her listed past employment and the businesses either no longer exist or never existed," Ryan said.

"This definitely seems like she's hiding something," Heather said. "But what?"

"And how does it relate to her death?" asked Peters.

"What's the best lead you have so far?" Chief Chet asked as he began to pet Miss Marshmallow again.

"The love note," Amy said quickly.

"There are no fingerprints on it, and it was written in block letters that are harder to trace to a certain writer," Ryan said.

"But it does prove that someone asked her to meet at the place she was killed," Heather said. "And because it was written on a heart, it looks like she had a romantic interest."

"Did anyone you spoke to mention a boyfriend?" Chief Chet asked, before saying to the dog. "You have the soft-iest woft-iest hair. Yes, you do."

Detective Peters bit his lip to keep from laughing.

"Her coworkers didn't mention a boyfriend, but they said that she was very private," Heather said. "And we haven't been able to track down many other people in her life."

"That's unfortunate," Chief Chet said to them, and then to Miss Marshmallow he said, "But what's not unfortunate is what a sweetie-petey pie you are."

"Who could have written that note?" Ryan wondered aloud.

"I'm pretty sure the answer is the killer," said Amy. "But I'm guessing we want a name too."

"Any other clues?" Chief Chet asked.

"The partial shoe prints," said Ryan. "And we found a hair, but it's not a match to anyone in the system."

"And there's the dog," Amy said.

"The dog," Heather said, getting an idea.

"The dog?" asked Detective Peters. "That was the only important thing in her life. Could Miss Marshmallow be valuable?"

"As a clue," said Heather. "It sounded as if Melanie Grayson had Miss Marshmallow since she moved here. Maybe if we can find out where Miss Marshmallow was adopted, it could tell us more about Melanie before she came here."

"That's a good idea," Ryan said. "Some rescue organizations and some breeders use tools that can help dogs be recognized if they are ever lost. Sometimes microchips are put on dogs or small tattoos."

"I don't think we'd see any tattoos on her with all her hair," said Amy.

"We can take her to the vet," Heather suggested. "And see if they can find anything to indicate where she came from."

"We'll continue to do some digging on Melanie Grayson's background here," Ryan said. "And let us know if you find anything that could help."

"No problem," Heather agreed.

"Then we have a plan of action. Yes, we do. Yes, we do," Chief Chet said, slipping into his baby talk voice again. He cleared his throat. "Let's get to work."

Chapter 10 – A Visit to the Vet

"Thank you for seeing us on such short notice," Heather said to the vet.

"I always take emergency calls when needed. And helping the police identify a dog for an investigation sounds important," Dr. Fisher said.

She was a middle-aged woman with her long hair in a braid down her back. She wore a white lab coat over her clothes but decorated it with buttons of dog treats.

"Though I don't think I'm going to need to do much work to

recognize this dog," Dr. Fisher said. "Isn't that Miss Marshmallow?"

"It is," Heather agreed.

"Then did something happen to her owner?" Dr. Fisher asked. She paused for a moment and then said, "Melanie, right? I'm always better with pet names than human ones. Sorry. Is she all right?"

"I'm afraid that Melanie Grayson was murdered," Heather said. "We're trying to find out more about her background and thought that maybe Miss Marshmallow could lead us down the right track."

Miss Marshmallow greeted the vet with a formal sniff of her hand.

"What can I do?" the vet asked.

"We'd like to find out where Miss Marshmallow was adopted from," said Heather. "Is there any way you can check?"

Dr. Fisher nodded and checked her file on the dog. "She didn't list where she adopted her from on her forms. Sometimes owners like to mention it in case any health problems could be related back to where they came from. Sometimes owners don't like to think about where their pups came from, or they forget the name of the organization."

"Is there anything else you can do?" asked Heather.

"Yeah," Amy said. "We'd really like to be done with this case."

"I have a scanner," Dr. Fisher said. "Let me see if Miss Marshmallow was ever given a microchip."

Dr. Fisher did as she said and checked the dog. She frowned as she saw something.

"What's wrong?" asked Heather.

"Everything is okay with Miss Marshmallow, isn't it?" asked Amy.

"She's fine and healthy," Dr. Fisher reassured her. "And she does have a microchip. I checked in against a database, and it looks like it was given to her by the Helping Paws and Pads Organization in Atlanta."

"That sounds like lead," Heather said, cheerfully.

"But there's something funny about it," Dr. Fisher said. "It also lists the name of the person who adopted her, and it's not Melanie Grayson."

"So, Miss Marshmallow was stolen?" Amy asked.

Miss Marshmallow barked indignantly.

"Sorry," Amy said quickly as if she had offended the dog.

"The name listed here is Mallory Gray," said Dr. Fisher. "I don't know why it would be listed under another name. All I can tell you is that it was."

"Thank you for all your help," Heather said.

She and Amy collected Miss Marshmallow and walked away.

"That wasn't such a bad vet visit, was it?" Amy asked the dog. "No shots or anything."

"Careful," Heather teased her friend. "Once you start talking to the dog, it won't be long until you start sounding like Chief Chet."

Amy groaned. "If I start doing that, you can push me into the ocean."

Miss Marshmallow was looking at them curiously.

"But I am starting to feel bad for her," Amy said. "I think her owner mom really loved her and took care of her. This must be a big change, and she must really miss her. I hope her new home will be just as loving."

"I'm sure it will be," Heather said, keeping any further comments or hunches to herself.

"What do you think of this Mallory Gray business?" Amy asked.

"Well," Heather said. "I can't help but notice that Mallory Gray and Melanie Grayson do sound very similar."

"So, you think that one of them is a fake name?" Amy asked. "And it's not that Miss Marshmallow was stolen from someone else, but that Melanie and Mallory are the same person."

"I think Ryan should do a background check on both women and see what turns up," Heather said.

It seemed as if Miss Marshmallow nodded at this idea.

***

"You were on to something," Ryan said. "I asked the Helping Paws and Pads Organization if they had any information about the people who adopted their pets."

"And?" Heather prompted. She and Amy had returned to the police station with Miss

Marshmallow to hear if their tip developed into a helpful lead.

"They take pictures of all their new adoptions," Ryan said. "Look at this."

He brought the photo they had emailed him up on the computer. It showed Melanie Grayson smiling with a young Miss Marshmallow puppy.

"That's definitely her," Heather said. "And the adoption was listed under Mallory Gray?"

"That's right," said Ryan. "And I believe that's the victim's real name. She changed her identity when she came here to escape her past."

"What sort of past is it?" Amy asked, eager for details. "Is it dark and sordid?"

"It seems Mallory Gray was arrested several times for petty theft," said Ryan.

"Wow," Amy said. "I didn't expect that."

"I guess as Melanie Grayson she was leading a clean life here," said Heather. "No one we spoke to mentioned any problems with her."

"But would petty theft be cause for murder?" Amy asked.

"Maybe someone here didn't like that she kept a secret," Heather said. "Or maybe someone from her past didn't like that she was running away from it."

"Or," Ryan said. "Maybe she was involved with something bigger right before she left. She would need money in order to reinvent herself and get a house in Key West."

"Were there any signs of other riches in her home?" asked Heather.

"No," Ryan admitted. "But it's something I want to investigate further. I'm going to do some more digging on Mallory Gray."

"All right," Heather said. "I have some more digging that I would like to do too. I had the feeling that Kim McConnell had something else that she wanted to tell us, but that she couldn't in front of her boss."

"So, we'll have to visit her during her off hours?" Amy asked.

"And I think she'll be off now," Heather said with a smile.

Chapter 11 – Coworker Gossip

Heather and Amy knocked on Kim McConnell's door. She seemed surprised to see them again.

"Hello," she said. "Do you have any new developments? Did you need to talk to me again? I thought Junior told you everything about Melanie at work."

"Not everything," Heather said. "Would you mind answering a few more questions?"

"I want to help, but I don't want to go against my bosses either. I'm sure they told you everything that's important," Kim said.

She started to close the door.

"Wait," Amy said. "There's something else. Miss Marshmallow has been so upset since she lost her owner. Maybe seeing a familiar face would help."

She held up the dog, and they both made their version of puppy dog eyes at her. Kim relented and opened the door.

"Come on in," Kim said.

She led them into her living room, which was a splash of color and personality. She gestured for Heather and Amy to take seats on her couch, which they accepted. Then, Kim sat right down on the floor to play with Miss Marshmallow. The happy dog accepted her affection.

"Thank you," Amy said. "I think it's really good for her to have some time with people she already knew."

"It must be so hard for her without Melanie," Kim said.

"I think so," said Heather. "And that's why we're trying so hard to find out what happened to her."

"I can't believe she was killed," Kim said. "Who would do that?"

"Do you have any idea who might have wanted to hurt her?" asked Heather.

Kim shrugged. "As I said before, she was quiet about her life outside of work. She was little quiet about her life at work too. But I didn't think there was anything to it that would be dangerous."

"So, she never spoke about a boyfriend?" Heather asked.

"No," Kim said. "She never spoke about one. I had a suspicion about something, but I ended up being wrong. Oh, my goodness!"

Miss Marshmallow jumped away from her after her exclamation and hid under a chair. Kim tried to coax her out again, but Heather wanted to hear more.

"What is it?" Heather asked.

"I just remembered why I was wrong and it might actually be a lead. Maybe that guy was the one who killed her. He seemed kinda crazy and kinda scary," Kim said.

"You're going to have to start at the beginning," Amy said.

"Sorry," Kim said. "I'll try and make more sense."

"That's appreciated," said Amy.

"I had thought that there might be something between Melanie and Jason Burdey," Kim explained. "It was just the way that they looked at each other. And a sense I got."

"Maybe he's the guy who wrote the heart message?" Amy said to her friend.

"What was that?" asked Kim.

"Nothing," Amy said quickly. She didn't want to reveal any information early again.

"So, you thought there was something between Melanie and Jason?" Heather prompted. "But they weren't officially dating?"

"They weren't dating," Kim said. "I had thought that but then I remembered why I was wrong."

"Which was?" asked Amy.

"Because of the guy who visited at work. I think it was her ex-boyfriend," Kim said. "Melanie tried not to make a big deal of it, but she did say that she was done with men. She only wanted her dog for company."

"When did this happen?" asked Heather.

"A week or two ago," Kim said. "We were at work, and this guy came in. He looked a little bit like a lowlife, but I thought he might be a customer so I was nice. He pushed by me and told Melanie that she couldn't hide from him. She said it was over and she didn't want to have anything to do with him. They went outside and talked for a while. She came back in all upset."

"Had you ever seen this man before?" Heather asked.

"No," said Kim. "And I got the sense that he wasn't from the island. He seemed like he was from out of town."

"But he was definitely her ex-boyfriend?" Amy asked.

"That's what it seemed like," said Kim.

"Maybe it's from before," Amy said, trying to speak in code to her friend. She didn't want to mention the past life and thefts in front of the witness.

"Do you know his name or where we might find him?" asked Heather.

"I think she might have called him Scratch," Kim said. "But I'm not sure if that's his name or an insult."

"Might be both," said Amy.

"I don't know how to contact him or if he's still in town. But he had longish dirty blond hair and a scar on his cheek. Is that helpful?"

"Maybe," said Heather. "Distinguishing markings are always useful to know about."

"Is there anything else you want to know?" Kim asked.

"Just where you were on Monday between two and four," said Heather.

"I was still at work," said Kim. "That's not my short day, and I don't get out until five."

"Who else was there with you?" asked Heather.

"You want to check up on me?" Kim asked. "You think I'm a suspect?"

"We just need to check out everything," said Heather. "Can you please answer?"

"Both of the Burdey Brothers were there," said Kim. "And at the end of the day, Jason and I were working on a project together, so he knows I was there the whole time."

"Thank you for your help," Heather said.

Amy called to Miss Marshmallow who daintily followed them to the door.

"Do you want me to take care of the dog?" Kim asked.

"Huh?" Amy asked, surprised. "Why?"

"Because you said it might be good for her to be with familiar people," said Kim. "I could watch her for a few days until you get things figured out."

"That's a great offer," said Amy. "But I'm afraid she's in police protection. We can't let her go until we solve this case."

Kim nodded. She wished them luck and said goodbye to Miss Marshmallow.

Heather gave her friend a look as they left.

"This doesn't mean I like the dog more," said Amy. "I'm just accepting my responsibilities."

"Sure," said Heather.

"Can we just focus on the case?" Amy asked.

"All right," said Heather. "Let's focus on finding the ex-boyfriend."

Chapter 12 – Scratch

Finding Scratch had been both easy and difficult depending on how you looked at it. The name Jordan "Scratch" Wilkerson had turned up in a search of Mallory Gray's past. They had been convicted of shoplifting together. Once they found this out, they were able to get his mugshot and saw how it matched Kim's description of the man who bothered Melanie at the office. The scar on his cheek was quite distinctive.

They then began questioning local hotels about whether the man had been staying there. At one hotel, they didn't need to

question the concierge behind
the desk because Scratch was
heading to the vending machine
as they approached. He didn't
like being questioned by the
police and tried to run.

Ryan and Peters had given
chase, while Amy held on to Miss
Marshmallow who was being
rather unladylike and had begun
snarling at Scratch.

Heather saw the direction that
Scratch was heading and had an
idea. She had delivered donuts to
this hotel before and knew where
the local streets intersected. She
raced down a side street, hoping
that her hunch was right and that

she wasn't sprinting for no reason.

Her gut proved her right, and she ended up in front of Scratch. She wanted to yell at him to stop but was too out of breath. She took her Taser out of her purse and held it out threateningly. Scratch took the hint and stopped running. Ryan and Peters were able to catch him and bring him back to the station.

Scratch was now sitting in the interrogation room, while Heather, Amy, Ryan and a miffed Miss Marshmallow looked through the two-way mirror at the suspect.

"Well, I certainly got my workout today," Heather said. "I'm not too happy about that, but that doesn't mean that he's guilty."

"Miss Marshmallow doesn't like him," Amy said. "I think he might have done it."

Miss Marshmallow growled again.

"We can't bring her into the interrogation room," Ryan said. "Not like that."

"I bet the chief will watch her," Heather said with a smirk.

Chief Chet did agree to watch the "widdle tweasure," and the others went into the room to talk to Scratch. Amy sat down and got ready to take notes, while Heather and Ryan sat down and faced the man.

"I didn't do anything," Scratch said. "Why am I here?"

"If you didn't do anything, why did you run away from us instead of speaking to us?" asked Ryan.

"Because cops are always causing trouble for me," Scratch said.

"Do you think maybe that has something to do with the robberies you were a part of?" Heather asked.

"I haven't done nothing recently, and you're threatening me with tasers," he said in a huff.

"Mr. Wilkerson, we'd like to talk to you about Melanie Grayson," said Ryan.

"Who?" he asked.

"You would know her as Mallory Gray," Heather said.

"What about her?" asked Scratch. "Is she trying to blame something on me? She always tried to do that. Anything to save her own skin."

"Well, it didn't work this time," said Amy.

"What was that?" asked Scratch.

"I'm afraid Miss Gray slash Miss Grayson is dead," said Heather.

"She was murdered," said Ryan. "And we'd like to find out who did it."

"Mallory is dead?" Scratch asked. "I can't believe it. I just found her. I just talked to her last week."

"Yes. We heard about that," said Heather. "You went to her workplace and harassed her."

"That's not what happened," said Scratch. "I came to Key West to find her. It took a long time to track her down. She was using a

different name as you know. But I
remembered when we were
together how she talked about
her dream place to retire. I
eventually found her."

"And you came all the way here,"
Heather said. "What were you
expecting to happen?"

"I just wanted to talk to her about
old times," said Scratch. "But she
was ignoring me. So, I went to
her job because I didn't think
she'd be able to ignore me there."

"And after she rebuffed your
romantic attempts, you got upset
and decided to kill her?" asked
Heather.

"I didn't kill her," Scratch said. "I didn't kill anybody."

"Why did you track her down?" asked Ryan.

"Like I said, to talk about the good old days."

Detective Peters entered the interrogation room.

"You were right, partner," he said, laying a file in front of Ryan and Heather.

"Mr. Wilkerson, I've just obtained some interesting news," said Ryan.

"Oh really? And what is that? Your kid partner got invited to prom?" Scratch asked.

Peters looked mad but said, "No. He just found out that you belong back in jail."

"I didn't do anything," said Scratch.

"Oh really?" asked Ryan. "Because it looks like a liquor store in Atlanta was robbed for quite a bit of money, and the thieves match the description of both you and Miss Gray."

"I don't know what you're talking about," said Scratch.

"You've avoided getting caught for two years, but killing your partner is what finally led to your capture," said Ryan firmly.

"I didn't kill her," Scratch said, losing his swagger. "I might have done some of the other stuff. But I didn't kill Mallory, I swear."

"Why should we believe that?" asked Heather.

"Look. I'll tell you everything you want to know, but you're not going to pin a murder on me," Scratch said.

"Did you rob the liquor store?" Ryan asked.

"Yes," Scratch said, looking down. "Mallory and I did it. We decided that we kept getting in trouble for smaller things, so we might as well try something big. And we got a lot of money too. But then she started feeling all guilty about it. She said taking thousands of dollars was different from taking a perfume bottle."

"So, she left?" Ryan asked.

"I told her to get a pet to calm her down, but it didn't help. And then one day she just disappeared. And she took all the money too."

"I bet that made you mad," said Heather.

"Of course it did," Scratch said. "And I've been looking for her for two years because of it. Not every waking moment of the day, but I did search. And then I finally found her, but she wouldn't take my calls."

"So, what did you do?" asked Heather.

"I went to her job and made her talk to me," said Scratch.

"You wanted her back?" asked Peters.

"No," said Scratch. "I wanted my half of the money."

"But you didn't get it?" asked Heather. "That's why you're still in town."

"Right," said Scratch. "She said she didn't have it. She said she returned what she didn't use to move here. Can you believe that?"

"I believe that must have made you furious," Ryan said.

"I told her that she better come up with a plan to get me my share of the money or I was going to tell all her friends about who she really was," said Scratch.

"You were blackmailing her?" Peters asked.

"After what she did to me, she deserved it." Then Scratch amended, "But I didn't kill her. I thought I'd let her sweat for a week or so and then see what she came up with."

"Is that why you wanted to meet her in the park?" asked Heather.

"No," said Scratch. "I didn't set up a meeting. I didn't think she would have the money yet if she were living the straight and narrow life. I was just enjoying my time on the island, and was planning on meeting up with her soon."

"Were you enjoying the island Monday afternoon?" Ryan asked.

"Monday I hung out at my hotel for a while and then I went for drinks that night," Scratch said.

"Can anyone verify that statement?" asked Ryan.

"I don't know," said Scratch. "But it's the truth."

The investigators finished their interrogation and then discussed it in the hall.

"What do you think?" Heather asked.

"I have enough to hold him on robbery charges," said Ryan. "So we have some time to figure out if he's the killer or not."

"Miss Marshmallow didn't like him," Amy reminded them. "And dogs have a sixth sense about this sort of thing."

"She might not like him because he was someone that Melanie didn't like anymore," Heather pointed out. "And not because he's a killer."

"Or she might not like him because she senses that he strangled her owner," Amy rebutted.

"The hair we found at the scene isn't his," Peters said. "If he did jail time, then it would have shown up in our search."

"But the hair isn't necessarily related," Ryan said. "It's possible that the hair was lost earlier in the public area."

"Scratch certainly has a motive for killing her," Heather said. "But would he have written that note?"

They all pondered the possibilities.

Chapter 13 – Doggie Dinner Discussion

After figuring out what Miss Marshmallow ate, the next dinner was a lot calmer. She was content to eat at her bowl, and Dave found the food so disgusting that he left her alone.

Dave sat next to Ryan and laid his head on his foot. He wanted to be nearby to the dinner table to collect scraps, but it also seemed like he wanted some manly moral support. It was as if he was saying in his own doggie way, "You were able to impress Heather? How? How do I impress this lady dog?"

Ryan was focusing on his tacos and was not much help. Amy and Jamie had joined them for their meal, and they had all listened to Lilly tell them about her day. She had kicked a scoring run during a kickball game and thought she was making new friends. She still missed her best friend from Hillside, Texas but thought she might ask some new friends over to play one day.

"We'd love to meet them," Heather said.

"Just as long as they don't stay here and never leave like our Miss Marshmallow guest," teased Amy.

Jamie had been quiet during most of the meal, and Amy turned to him. "Are you okay?"

"I just feel bad that this happened," said Jamie. "I was too focused on my business opening up, and I didn't realize that someone needed my help."

"There's no way you could have known," said Heather. "Just because it was by the park doesn't mean you could have heard it. And the killer made sure that no one was watching."

"You did everything you could afterward," said Amy.

"But I wish I could have done something before," said Jamie.

"It sounds as if Melanie Grayson was happy when she visited the van," Heather said. "And if she took the heart to be a real romantic invitation, then that makes sense."

"She was dressed up," said Jamie. "It might have been like she wanted to look nice for someone."

"She had no idea that he wanted to kill her," said Heather. "And because she had no inkling of it, there was no way that you could have been suspicious."

"Thanks," Jamie said. "I had been feeling bad about this."

"I've been telling you it's not your fault," Amy said.

"I know," Jamie said.

"But you had to hear it from Heather to believe it?" Amy asked with mock anger.

"Well," Jamie said. "You love me. You would say that."

"I thought I've been pretty clear that I speak my mind," Amy said, and everyone laughed.

"That's especially true when you let me know your feelings about the dog," said Jamie. "You think she's spoiled and entitled, and high-maintenance."

"Well," Amy said. "She's not too bad for a furball."

They were just about finished their meal, and Heather asked Lilly if she would mind bringing in the donuts.

"Not at all," Lilly said with a smile.

"And take your time," Amy said. "So we can have some murderous discussions."

Once Lilly was out of the room, Jamie asked, "Do you have any leads?"

"We discovered that Melanie Grayson was also Mallory Gray, a woman escaping from a robbery she committed," said Heather.

"But she did feel bad about it," said Amy. "It looked like she was trying to change her life, and she told her ex-partner that she returned most of the money."

"And her being on the run explains why her home and office were so bland," said Ryan. "She didn't want anything to give her away and trace back to who she really was."

"Do you think the partner did it?" asked Jamie.

"He certainly had a motive," said Heather. "And his alibi is very weak.

"Weak like a baby in an arm wrestling competition," said Amy. "Plus, Miss Marshmallow hates him."

"Dogs are very good at judging someone's character," Jamie noted.

"That's what I said!" said Amy.

"But," Heather said. "He admitted to everything else. Why not admit to the murder?"

"A murder charge is more serious," said Ryan. "Maybe he

thought we'd believe him more if he confessed to other things. It might make him look more sincere."

"He's not going to get any money from Melanie slash Mallory if she's dead," said Heather.

"But maybe she was never going to give him the money," said Ryan. "He got angry and used the leash that she was holding to carry out the deed. It might not have been premeditated."

"And the shoe prints?" asked Amy.

"They're only partials, so it's not definitive," said Ryan. "But his size feet could have made those marks."

"We're forgetting about the note though," said Heather. "It was written on a heart."

"Maybe Scratch was being mean," said Amy.

"No," said Heather. "She thought it was from someone that she liked and trusted. Otherwise, she would have been nervous about the meeting."

"She didn't look nervous," said Jamie. "She looked happy."

"So, maybe Scratch wrote the note pretending to be somebody else," said Amy.

"Maybe," said Heather. "But then who did Melanie Grayson think the note was from?"

"We still need to find the lover," Amy said.

"Exactly," said Heather. "And I think looking at the office again is a good place to start."

Lilly returned with the dessert and Heather handed out the Cranberry Glazed Donuts. Everyone was very grateful for their yummy snacks, except for Miss Marshmallow. She turned

her nose up and it and swatted it
away.

The donut piece landed near
Dave, and he happily ate it. He
both loved the snack and thought
it was a token of love. He headed
over to Miss Marshmallow who
stopped looking bored and hid
behind Lilly.

"She really doesn't like donuts?"
asked Heather.

"That's the strangest part of this
case," said Amy.

Chapter 14 – Back to the Office

"Back again?" Kim asked as she saw the investigators enter the office. "Did one of our buildings have something to do with Melanie's death?"

"No. It doesn't look that way," said Ryan. "All of your clients do appear to be happy, and the buildings are designed to code."

"That's good to hear," said Kim.

"Yeah," Amy said. "You could probably use that endorsement in a review."

"But something here does have something to do with her death?"

asked Kim. "Besides the building plans?"

"Possibly," Ryan said. "That's what we're here to find out."

Kim looked at the four investigators solemnly. "I want to help, but I don't know what to say. Did you find her ex?"

"Yes," said Ryan. "And he is a viable suspect, but there are still some loose ends that we need to tie up."

"Firstly, did you see Scratch any other times besides when he showed up that day at the office?" asked Peters.

"No," said Kim. "I only saw him here once."

"Maybe he really was just sipping margaritas on the beach instead of killing anyone," said Amy. "Or maybe he was staying out of sight before he completed his kill."

"You said that you were here all Monday afternoon?" asked Heather.

"That's right," said Kim. "And both of my bosses can verify that. Junior was in his office a lot, and Jason was on the phone. But they were both there."

"The last thing we need to know about is the romance that you suspected," said Ryan.

Kim blushed. "I think I was all wrong about that though. I don't want to spread gossip if it's false."

"You're not gossiping," Heather assured her. "You're expressing your observations. We'll make sure we validate anything before we use it as evidence. But telling us what you thought of Melanie's behavior will be helpful. Everything is in a murder case."

"Okay," Kim said. "But as I said, I think I was wrong about it now. Because Melanie was always so private and shy. And then after that visit from her ex, she said she was done with men."

"But before that?" Ryan prompted.

"I thought that she and Jason were into each other," she said. "They'd smile a little too much when they saw each other. And the way they spoke to each other, I thought there were feelings there."

"But they never officially said that they were dating?" asked Peters.

"No," said Kim. "But they wouldn't have told me anyway. Why is this so important?"

"We found a note written on a piece of heart-shaped paper," Ryan said. "We want to know who sent it to the victim, and who she thought she was meeting."

"I don't remember seeing a note like that," said Kim. "And I don't know if Jason would send anything like that."

"What's going on here?" Junior Burdey asked, bursting into the middle of their group. "I really must protest this."

"Protest what?" asked Amy.

"You keep coming here and bothering my employees. We're trying to run a business, and we're a person short," Junior said.

"We know," said Amy. "That's kinda why we're here. To find out what happened to her."

"I gave you all the paperwork I had on her," said Junior. "And I allowed you to take what she had on her desk. That is truly all the help we can offer. I know her death had nothing to do with us."

"How can you know that?" asked Heather.

"Because we are a reputable business and have nothing to do with murderers," said Junior. "Now, please, I'd like you to leave. You being here might make my brother sick again."

"Where is your brother?" Ryan asked. "We'd like to talk to him."

"There's no reason for that," said Junior. "Even if someone was repeating untrue gossip about him."

"Then why was he so sick when we were first here?" asked Amy.

"Because he was saddened and repulsed to learn that our employee was dead," said Junior. "He was the one who hired the woman, and I think he felt responsible for her."

"How thorough a background check did you do on her?" Heather asked.

"I'm not sure," said Junior. "My brother handled that at the time, but she was a very capable worker while she was here."

"Then we'd like to speak to him even more," said Peters.

"Look, we're all very upset about what happened to Mallory, but that's no excuse to shut down our business and try and accuse my brother," Junior said. "He'll talk to you if he sees fit, and until then I want you to go."

"No," Jason said, overhearing and joining them. "I'll speak with them."

"You don't have to," Junior said.

"Yes. I do," said Jason. "We should all do whatever we can to catch this killer."

"That's an attitude I like to hear," said Amy.

Jason nodded and led them to his office.

Chapter 15 – An Office Romance?

"I'm sorry I couldn't speak with you the first time you visited," Jason said.

"We've been sickened by murder before," said Amy. "Though not quite as literally."

Then she set up to take notes, as Heather began the questioning.

"If you were so upset by her death, would you say that you and Melanie were close?" Heather asked.

"She worked here about two years," Jason responded.

Heather realized she was going to have to go slow to get Jason to open up about his relationship with the victim.

"And you were the one who hired her?"

"Yes," said Jason. "She was eager to find a job so she could stay in Key West. I can't begrudge her that. And she seemed to really enjoy it here."

"You didn't do a background check on her?" Ryan asked.

"There was no need," said Jason. "I could tell right away that there was something special about her.

She wanted to learn, and she had a good resume."

"But you didn't contact any of her old places of employment?" Ryan asked.

"No," Jason said. "I could already tell she was the right candidate. And I was right. She was great here. She thrived."

"But she didn't talk about herself much?" Heather asked.

"That's right," said Jason. "She was a quiet person, but very dedicated. And she had wonderful instincts. She could have been an architect herself, but she said she didn't want to apply to school and take the classes."

Heather nodded. If Melanie Grayson was lying about her identity, she probably didn't want to take any chances where her background might be looked up.

Jason continued. "She was nervous. I got the sense that she didn't have a happy life before she came here."

"That's one way of looking at it," said Amy.

"She was looking for something better and hoped to find it in the sand and the sun," Jason said.

"She helped us make other people their dream homes, and I think that made her glad."

"Mr. Burdey, were you and Melanie dating?" Heather asked.

"No," Jason said quickly. "Well, we weren't. But I hoped we might."

"You liked her?" Heather asked, giving him a smile of encouragement to continue.

"I think I fell in love with her the first moment I saw her," Jason said. "And through our time working together, I think she liked me too. Recently, she had begun to open up to me a little more. I was planning on asking out to her dinner soon and seeing if there was a way we could be together and still work together. I think she really liked her job. Sometimes I thought she liked it because I was there, but other times I thought that idea was arrogant. But I loved her, and that's why I was so upset when I heard she was gone."

"When you said she started to open up you, what did she say?" asked Heather.

"Little things. But it was still wonderful to know more about her likes and dislikes. She was so private at first. But then she did tell me that she had a big secret.

Apparently, a man bothered her at work while I was out. He's lucky I was out."

"What would you have done?" asked Peters.

"I would have called the police and had him hauled to jail," Jason admitted. "I'm no fighter. But I would have done more than what was done. No one should have been able to bother her like that. I think her secret had something to do with that man. And I know she wanted to tell me what it was. She told me that we would talk soon."

"Then things were getting more serious," Heather said.

"I hoped so," Jason said. "I have a secret too. Telling you will either make me look crazier or more innocent."

"What is it?" asked Ryan.

"I bought a ring," Jason said.

"Like a wedding ring?" Amy asked. "For a woman you never even went on a date with? I need to tell Jamie to step up his game and get me one."

Heather raised an eyebrow at her friend.

"I'm kidding," Amy said.

"We hadn't dated, but we did know each other. And we understood each other. I know we would have loved each other," Jason said. "And I wasn't going to spring it on her right away. But I was certain about her, so I kept it in my desk drawer."

"Were you the one who left her the heart note?" asked Heather.

"What heart note?" asked Jason.

"We found a note in her desk asking her to meet someone at the park when she got off of work Monday," Ryan said. "Was that you?"

"No," Jason said. "I had to work after she left. I wouldn't have left a note like that."

"Is it possible she thought the note was from you?" Ryan asked.

"Was it written in block letters?" Jason asked.

"Yes," Ryan said.

"Then it is possible," Jason said. "I told her how I used to write letters in block writing to someone I had a crush on in school. She might have thought I was doing the same thing now. Did someone use our feelings for each other to lure her to her death?"

"It might be a coincidence," Ryan said. "Someone could have just written it that way to disguise their handwriting."

"Or you could have written it," Peters said. "You didn't like what she told you about her past, and so you killed her."

"That's ridiculous," Jason Burdey said. "I was at work all that afternoon."

"You didn't leave at all?" Heather asked.

"No," said Jason. "I was working on a project all day. I had lunch brought in that afternoon, and I was working straight through.

Kim was there. She helped me at the end of the day."

"Still," Peters said. "The romantic interest is always a strong suspect."

"What do you want from me?" Jason asked. "Do you want a handwriting sample? My blood type? DNA to test? I would never hurt her. Whatever you want, I'll give it to you."

"Well," Amy said. "Since you're offering, we'll accept."

Chapter 16 – Biting Accusations

"This walk is calmer than I expected," Amy said to her bestie.

Miss Marshmallow was joining in on their walk with Dave and Cupcake. At first, Dave had been trying to impress her by pointing out all the good things to smell. However, he lost enthusiasm when she bared her teeth at him. He began to sniff the grass with his friend Cupcake instead.

"And she's actually walking," said Amy. "I was afraid I'd have to carry her around the whole time."

Miss Marshmallow began to pick up the pace as if she understood and was indignant with the remark. Heather and Amy hurried along.

"I guess she's not so bad," Amy said.

"I'm sorry I've been distracted during the walk," Heather said. "You're right. She's a good dog."

"I didn't go that far in my compliments," Amy joked. "And I understand your distraction. This happens when we're close to solving a case, but also we feel far away from answers."

"When Ryan gets the results of the DNA test back from the lab, we can see if Jason Burdey is the prime suspect," Heather said.

"If it matches, it helps," said Amy. "But Ryan and Peters keep reminding us not to get ahead of ourselves. The hair could have been lost by someone in the park earlier in the day. If it doesn't match, then Jason Burdey could still be the killer."

"He does have an alibi," Heather said. "If we believe Junior and Kim that he was at work all afternoon. Jason said that he and Kim were working on a project together at the end of the workday."

"She did tell us that without being prompted," Amy said, thinking. "But I bet both of them would cover for him. They wouldn't want him to be accused of murder."

"He was the person that Melanie slash Mallory liked," said Heather. "She thought the heart note was from him."

"But was it?" asked Amy. "Did he write it and lie about it? Or did someone else leave the note and she just thought it was from him?"

"And if someone else wrote it," Heather thought aloud. "Did they mean for the message to look like it came from Jason Burdey? Or were they just sending their message on a heart so that it didn't look threatening?"

"These are very good questions," said Amy. "And I don't have any answers."

They continued walking. Miss Marshmallow was starting to look at the way Dave and Cupcake were enjoying strolling next to one another.

"Who do you think did it?" Heather asked.

"Scratch," said Amy. "He had the best motive. He and the victim were partners and she stole his share of the loot. He was really mad about it. He searched for her and followed her across the country to get the money."

"But he's never going to get the money now that she's dead," said Heather.

"Then it was just a vengeance killing," said Amy. "When he saw her again, he was so mad that needed revenge and he strangled her."

"Maybe," said Heather.

"Well, then who do you think it was?" asked Amy.

Heather sighed. "I don't know. There are some things that point to Scratch, but it doesn't seem cut and dry to me. But our other suspect, Jason Burdey, has an alibi. They both had reasons to be mad at the secrets Melanie kept."

"Or Mallory kept," said Amy.

"But I don't know who the strangler is."

Miss Marshmallow seemed to be getting jealous of how content Dave and Cupcake were. She moved closer to them and joined in on sniffing everything that they did. Dave wagged his tail heartily.

They continued their walk in this happy formation. Heather wasn't too distracted by unanswered questions in the case to ignore the doggie dynamics. She smiled at their antics, and when the finished their route, they returned home. Ryan had just arrived home too.

"It's good to see you," Heather said, giving him a kiss.

"Are the animals getting along?" Ryan asked.

"Better than expected," said Amy.

"Do you have any news?" Heather asked, wanting to hear more about the case.

"Well, we ran the DNA test that Jason Burdey suggested," Ryan said.

"And was it a match?"

"That's the strange part," said Ryan. "It was only a partial match."

"A partial match?" asked Amy. "Does that make any sense?"

Suddenly the pieces all fit into place in Heather's mind. "It makes perfect sense."

"How?" asked Amy.

"He called her Mallory," Heather said, hitting herself in the forehead. "Why didn't I realize it before?"

"Yeah," said Amy. "Why did you realize before? And why don't you tell me now?"

Chapter 17 – Facing the Killer

"I should stop saying "You're back!" and being surprised about it," Kim said, as Heather and Amy entered the office.

"Unfortunately, we're still not here about building a dream house," said Amy.

"Then you know who the killer is?" Kim asked. "Was I helpful? Are you going to catch him partly because of me? It was that crazy ex of hers, right?"

"What you told us was very helpful," said Heather. "And you can continue to help us some more."

"Did you decide you do want me to take Miss Marshmallow? Because I could really only take her for a few days," Kim said. "I can't take care of her forever. I loved when she visited the office, but I'm really more of a cat person."

"No. We don't need you to take Miss Marshmallow," Amy assured her.

"Then what?"

"We need you to think back to the day of the murder," Heather said. "You were working here?"

"That's right. I was here all afternoon with the Burdey Brothers," Kim said.

"That's what I need you to focus on," said Heather. "Now you said you were working on a project with Jason Burdey."

"We were working on our own things at first," said Kim. "I had some permits to look over before they were mailed. But then we did work on something together. It must have been around three-thirty. And we worked on it for the rest of the day."

"What was Jason doing before that?" asked Heather.

"He was drawing a new design and was in and out of his office. He always wanders when he does that. And he was making some phone calls too," said Kim.

"So, you definitely saw him in the building?" Heather said.

"Of course," said Kim.

"What about Junior Burdey?"

"Well, he…" Kim trailed off as she thought about it. "He was in his office. And he had his door closed after lunch for a while."

"So, you didn't actually see him?" Heather asked.

"No," Kim said. "I guess I didn't."

Heather nodded and made a quick call to Ryan. Her hunch was right.

"All right, Kim," Amy said. "I think you're going to want to leave the building for a bit."

"Why?" Kim asked.

"Trust us," said Amy. "We think you might not want to be here."

"What's going on?" Junior Burdey asked, striding towards them. "How long is this going to go on?"

"I don't know," Amy shrugged. "Twenty to life?"

"What?" Junior asked.

"Nothing," said Heather, nudging her friend. They needed to wait for the police to arrive and make the arrest. She didn't want Junior Burdey to flee and for her to have to give chase to a suspect again.

"Junior, you didn't have anything to do with Melanie's death, did you?" Kim asked.

Heather groaned inwardly. She didn't want Junior to know that they were on to him.

"How could I have?" Junior asked. "I was here at work with you the whole time. Wasn't I?"

Kim's gaze dropped to the floor.

"Well," Junior said, covering. "If we're not going to get any work done today, I might as well go home."

He headed to his desk in his office and began to pack up.

"We have to stall him," Heather whispered.

"How?" asked Amy.

Heather walked up to his desk, trying to block his escape.

"What are you doing?" he asked.

"Would you like to hear my theory about how the killer committed his crime?" Heather asked.

"I'm sure it would be riveting," Junior said. "But I'd rather wait and hear what the police have to say than listen to some private investigator."

"Don't worry," Amy said. "The police will be here soon."

"And why are they coming here?" Junior asked. "Besides to interrupt our work."

"Did you know that your brother volunteered to give us a DNA sample to clear his name?" Heather asked.

"What?" Junior asked.

"We compared his sample to a hair that was found at the scene, but it was only a partial match. Why was it partial?" Heather asked. "Because it wasn't from him, but it did belong to a family member of his."

"Are you trying to say it was me?" Junior asked. "That's crazy. I was here at work."

"You said you were here," Heather said. "But you just closed your office door, and that allowed you the chance to leave through your window and strangle your employee."

"Why would I kill Mallory?"

"Aha," Amy said. "That was your big mistake. You just did it again."

"What?"

"You called her Mallory instead of Melanie," Heather said. "And I'm guessing that the reason you killed her had something to do with finding out her past. You found out about Mallory Gray's thefts. Once you knew her real name, it was hard to keep track of what to call her."

"Circumstantial," Junior said.

However, before he could leave, he was stopped by Ryan and

Detective Peters. They read him his rights on their way to the door.

Junior decided to waive his right to be silent and shouted, "Circumstantial. It's all circumstantial! You don't have anything on me. I didn't kill Mallory."

Jason Burdey entered the room and saw his brother being arrested.

"Mallory?" Jason asked. "Who's Mallory? Why are you being arrested?"

Junior just couldn't contain it anymore. "You idiot," he said. "I did all of this for you, and you have no idea."

"Did what?" Jason asked.

"I was saving you from yourself," Junior said.

"Who's Mallory?"

"Mallory is who Melanie really was," Junior nearly spat at his brother. "She was a thief who lied about everything."

"That can't be true," Jason said.

"You were so head over heels for her that you couldn't see the truth, but I did the research. She was a robber and a con artist.

She was a liar," said Junior. "And you bought her a ring."

"How did you know that?" Jason asked.

"I saw it in your desk. I knew you were going to make the biggest mistake of your life, and I knew you wouldn't listen to anything that I said. So, I did what I always do. I took care of you. I saved you," Junior said.

"By killing Melanie?"

"The thief Mallory."

"You wrote that note telling her to go to the park, so she thought it was from me," Jason said. "You

used our love as a trap and killed
her."

"You should be thanking me,"
Junior said.

"I told you before I wasn't much
of a fighter," Jason said.
"Officers, can you take him
away?"

Ryan and Detective Peters
obliged and took him away.
Jason looked down-trodden.

"Are you going to be sick again?"
Amy asked.

"No," Jason said. "I'm not. And I
don't care what Junior says.
Melanie, or whoever she was,

wasn't bad. And she wasn't trying to con me. She was trying to start over. She was going to tell me about her past, and I would have forgiven her. We would have been happy together. Our feelings were real."

"I believe you," Heather said.

Kim hugged Jason and suggested they take the rest of the day off.

Heather and Amy left the two coworkers to deal with the loss of their friend and the repercussions of discovering the killer.

"Well, the murderer was caught," Heather said. "There's just one

more question that needs
answering."

"What's that?"

"What's going to happen to Miss
Marshmallow?"

Amy groaned.

Chapter 18 – Dog Decisions

"Do we have enough room for everyone?" Lilly asked.

"We'll make room if we need to," Heather assured her daughter.

They were going to have a movie night that evening and the whole gang was attending. The Shepherds, Amy and Jamie, and Eva and Leila would be there. While this was the usual large gathering of humans, there would also be Miss Marshmallow joining the animal guest list.

Lilly was selecting a movie when they heard Amy and Jamie arriving with the dog. Miss

Marshmallow allowed Dave to sniff her for a moment and then headed to her favorite person, Lilly.

"How has business been?" Heather asked.

"It's been good," Jamie said with a smile. "People have been pretty pleased with their pet's grooming."

"That's wonderful," said Heather.

"Just as long as none of my business relates to one of your murder cases again," said Jamie. "Then I'll be very happy."

"Let's bring out some celebratory donuts," Heather said. "Jamie's Mobile Groom Room is going strong, and we solved our case in time for our outing tomorrow."

Lilly leaped up and grabbed the donuts. The humans all took a Cranberry Glazed Donut and enjoyed the snack.

"I love celebratory donuts," Amy said. "But I love every type of donut."

"I don't think you'll love these ones," Heather said, showing her friend a smaller batch.

"What are they? Why not?"

"These are some doggie donuts that I whipped up," Heather said. "I tried to match some ingredients from Miss Marshmallow's food so she would feel more at home."

Heather gave each of the pets one of her new donuts. Cupcake played with hers and then happily ate it. Dave ate his in one big bite and then looked around for more.

Amy ventured a bite of the dog donuts and said, "Actually, they're not bad either."
Miss Marshmallow just stared at hers. Heather tried not to be too disappointed.

"It's okay," Heather said. "Some foods just aren't for everyone."

"With a name like Miss Marshmallow, she's not really that sweet," Amy commented.

"But what is going to happen to Miss Marshmallow?" Lilly asked.

"Well," Heather said. "It doesn't appear that Mallory Gray had any more family that Melanie Grayson did. There's no family to inherit the dog."

"I did ask Jason Burdey if he wanted to take Miss Marshmallow home, but he said that he thought it would make him too sad. She would be a constant reminder of what he lost," Amy said. "And you heard that Kim says she's more of a cat person."

Heather nodded.

"Right," Lilly said. "But then who is going to take care of her?"

"We don't know," Amy said.

"What?" asked Lilly. "That's not an answer."

Amy looked at Jamie and then at the others. "Well, we don't know yet. But Jamie and I have agreed to foster Miss Marshmallow until we can find the perfect home for her."

"But you're not going to keep her?" Lilly asked. "It seems like fate that she was left with you when all this bad stuff happened."

"And it was," said Amy. "We're going to be great foster parents until she finds her forever home. But we're not quite ready to get our own dog yet. Jamie just started a business, and I'm always busy too."

Jamie nodded, though with less enthusiasm.

"And besides," Amy said. "Miss Marshmallow is nice, but she doesn't really fit in with us. She doesn't even like donuts!"

Miss Marshmallow had begun staring at her snack and regarding it with curiosity. She finally took a little bite of it. She immediately perked up and wagged her tail. She practically danced around with glee as she finished it. It was the first time that they had seen her truly happen after her ordeal, and Heather was pleased that she could be a part of it.

If Heather had a tail, it would be wagging too.

The End.

A letter from the Author

To each and every one of my Amazing readers: I hope you enjoyed this story as much as I enjoyed writing it. Let me know what you think by leaving a review!

Stay Curious,
Susan Gillard

Made in United States
North Haven, CT
22 October 2022